Good Night Captain Mama

Buenas Noches Capitán Mamá

Written by Graciela Tiscareño-Sato

Illustrated by Linda Lens

Published by
Gracefully Global Group, LLC
Hayward, California

Gracefully Global Group

Cataloging Data

Tiscareño-Sato, Graciela.
Good Night Captain Mama / by Graciela Tiscareño-Sato : illustrated by Linda Lens
Summary: Five-year old Marco sees his Mama in her military flight suit;
his questions about the colorful patches spark a conversation about why mommies serve and wear uniforms.
Includes template for art activity for children to design their own patches for their team or school.

Buyers interested in the upcoming Premium Hardcover Library Edition, please inquire with the publisher at info@gracefullyglobal.com.

ISBN: 978-0-9834760-3-0 (Paperback)
ISBN: 978-0-9834760-4-7 (iBook)
ISBN: 978-0-9834760-5-4 (Kindle)

Library of Congress Control Number: 2013936046
Library of Congress Subject Headings
[1. Bilingual – Easy Picture. 2. Women air pilots – Fiction. 3. Air pilots, Military – Fiction.
4. Mothers and sons – Fiction. 5. Military service. Voluntary – Fiction.]

Printed in the United States

Book design by: Suzi Lee Musgrove of SLM Creative Design and Associates, San Rafael, CA
www.slmcreative.com

For more information about Gracefully Global Group, LLC
please visit our web site at www.gracefullyglobal.com.
22568 Mission Blvd. No. 427, Hayward, CA 94541

URL Disclaimer
All Internet addresses given in this book were valid at the time of going to press. However, due to the dynamic nature of the Internet, some addresses may have changed or sites may have changed or ceased to exist since publication. While the author and publisher regret any inconvenience this may cause readers, no responsibility for any such changes can be accepted by either the author or the publisher.

For the people who made my role as Mamá possible:
my husband Genro, our little man Kiyoshi, and my big girls Kotomi and Milagro. —Graciela

For my son Johnny and my daughter Saila, my two sweetest inspirations! —Linda

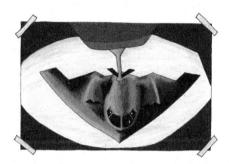

Acknowledgements

I'm deeply indebted to my illustrator **Linda Lens** for her ability to capture the love expressed in this story so perfectly through her art. In addition, the following team members played key roles in helping to birth this book: Translator **Anabel Granados** for expertly bringing the story into Spanish, my first language as a child; editor and publishing consultant **Ruth Schwartz** for her expertise in all things PCN, LOC, CIP, a keen eye for detail and language usage, and for coaching me through the print production process; preschool teacher **Patti Brohard** for editorial support and for teaching my three children; **Rosi Bustamante** for reviewing the manuscript in both English and Spanish and graphic designer **Suzi Lee Musgrove of SLM Creative** for bringing the words and art together so elegantly. To **Stacy Ingersoll**, thanks for helping me with the daily insanity and for keeping me organized. To **my parents, Arturo and Tina**, thank you for giving me roots and wings. To **Ivonne Luna de Thompson**, for your fresh eyes when it mattered the most. Lastly, to my husband **Genro**: thank you as always for the creative inputs, the scanning, the web parts and the countless other forms of support. Really, I could not have done this without you. —*Graciela*

Special thanks to **my parents** for their loving enthusiasm, as well as **my family**! Thank you **Danny Sychr** for your support and ideas. Thanks to everyone who said all the amazingly encouraging words; I took them all to heart! Thank you for believing in me. —*Linda*

Together with V-WISE: Supporting Women Veterans, Creating Entrepreneurs and Business Value

A portion of all sales of this book will be shared with V-WISE (Veteran Women Igniting the Spirit of Entrepreneurship), a project operated by the Institute for Veterans and Military Families (IVMF) at Syracuse University. V-WISE recognizes the leadership, integrity, focus and drive of women veterans and teaches business-savvy skills to turn their ideas or businesses into growth ventures. Learn more about V-WISE at whitman.syr.edu/vwise and the IVMF at vets.syr.edu.

We are grateful for the following supporters whose preorders and contributions helped to make this book possible:

Agustina Tiscareño
Cammie Herbert
Chantal Maherrajlich
Laura Edwards
Linda Falter
Heinrich Hartmann
Noriko Sato
Peggy Robles-Alvarado
Sergio Hernandez
Ikuko Sato
Alexander Gallegos
Ellen S. Silber
Sandra Westlie
Lynette Hoy
Rosa Oyarce
Martha Hernandez
Lyle Funderburk
Judy Rodriguez
Yesenia Flores
Victoria Hudson
Lydia White
Laura Ackley
Mimi Hernandez
Alma Renteria
Colleen Gilmartin
Karl Wieser
Michael Takamoto
Linda Liebman
Maryann Lens

Andre Hill
Virginia Winblad
Stephanie Gardner
Maria Sanchez
Jennifer Garcia
Daliana Rivera
Monica Bega
Neverest Solutions, LLC
Tammy Schinker Lewis
Helen Arias
Monica Alvarez
Star Lara, U.S. Army Veteran
Irma Herrera
Valerie Menard
Monica DeZulueta
RWR Innovations LLC
Catherine Luce
Linda Maloney
Gordon Smith
Ana Uribe-Ruiz
Cheryl Royer
Omar Valle
Diana Miller
Christy Schultz
Irma Castaneda
Lucy Macias
Victoria Ramirez
Eugenia Miranda
Jay Bae

Gini Fiero
Mary Boyd
Ann Matranga
Daniel Perry
CasaQ (Owner, Darlene Tenes)
Jeannine Churchill
Kerrin Torres-Meriwether
Stephane McCoy
Victoria Ramirez
Gina "Latina" Miranda
Jayne Zuhlke
Claudia Romero
Olivia Castro
Irasema Carranza
Gloria Perez-Stewart
Linda Meyer
Julia Arellano Sullivan
Angelica Perez-Litwin
Leadership Empowerment Group, LLC
Caroline Avakian
Sofia Colón
Wendy Sanchez
Alberto and Mary Lens
Federico Subervi
Theresa Jones
Wilson Lee
Ana and Sergio Medina
Crystal Ramirez

Praise for *Good Night Captain Mama*

"*Good Night Captain Mama* couldn't be more timely for a generation of children who live the reality of mothers serving in our nation's military. A book that was needed decades ago, this sweet story is sure to become a highly requested bedtime story that will send its readers and listeners into dreams of high flying missions! Tiscareño-Sato opens the door for children to relay their fears regarding parents who go off and serve. This book possibly gives children their very first glimpse into flying, the military, and a national pride for our service members. It also surely serves the unsung hero of the military, the military child, very well!"

–*Sheila Thompson, USAF Navigator, Girls with Wings Inc.*

. . . .

"*Good Night Captain Mama* beautifully captures the sweet, thoughtful questions our children ask. It also shares the legacy a mom is passing down to her son—a wonderful picture of patriotism, love of country and the love between a mom and her child. The illustrations are fabulous and make the book come alive!"

–*Linda Maloney, Author,* Military Fly Moms *& retired naval aviator*

. . . .

"This book is a treasure, a wonderful way for a child to learn about flight, about service, and to share in his mother's life and adventures... The Spanish translation for the English text is a welcome addition. Like many educators who have seen the positive results of dual-language learning, this was a particular delight for me... It also provides a vehicle for children to be proud of their heritage and culture and to see the beauty and interconnections between both languages. More people should know of the sacrifices that Latinos and Latinas have made (and are continuing to make) for the United States; too few do."

–*Dr. Michael Hogan, author of* The Irish Soldiers of Mexico.
Former State Department consultant for the Office of Overseas Schools

. . . .

"With war being an everyday topic in America, many families have children with questions they need answered and emotions they cannot translate to their parents. *Good Night Captain Mama* gives children an opportunity to connect with their parents and understand the patriotic duty Mommy or Daddy has that takes them away for weeks or months at a time. This book starts the conversation our children cannot start themselves."

–*Patricia Brohard, retired preschool teacher/proud Air Force mom*

Praise for *Good Night Captain Mama*

"As the father of four children who joined the Air Force, I wish I'd had this book to read to them while they were young. This book will help military parents explain to their children what they do, and why they sometimes have to go away."

–Ron Nixon, MSgt, USAF Retired; Owner, RWR Innovations, LLC

Your Melissa & Doug Store, Omaha, Nebraska, www.rwrinnovations.com

. . . .

"Poignant, powerful and beautiful—*Good Night Captain Mama* celebrates a mother's love for her child and a military woman's love for her country. As we turn the pages, we journey through that special and impressionable moment when a child rediscovers who his mother is, beyond 'Mom.' This enlightening story of courage, love and leadership is a must-have book on children's night tables and library bookshelves around the world."

–Angelica Perez-Litwin, *Founder of ELLA Leadership Institute, Publisher of* NEW LATINA

. . . .

"This is a book that I would recommend to any service member who is also a parent. It provides a positive outlook on female service members, gives children a better understanding of United States Air Force patches and the important role that mothers play in today's military."

–Tina M. Kapral, *Director of Education Programs,*

Institute for Veterans and Military Families at Syracuse University (IVMF)

. . . .

"A truly inspiring work – a beautiful reminder to nourish the curiosities of our youth, and to strive to make our most vibrant dreams a reality."

–Judy Rodriguez, *Library Information Specialist, Fremont, California*

Praise for *Good Night Captain Mama*

"Que maravilla de historia y que buen ejemplo para todos nuestros niños y niñas. Es una belleza ver como una familia militar funciona y como se puede enriquecer a esa nueva generación de madres profesionales."

–Ana Ruiz, pilota, banquera

. . . .

"El libro…con coloridas y encantadoras ilustraciones, presenta una fabulosa herramienta, para aquellas familias con mujeres militares, pero también para todos los niños en general, ya que es un tema muy actual y todos conocemos en este momento a alguien que está sirviendo activamente en las fuerzas armadas. Y no sólo eso, este es el primer y único libro bilingue sobre el tema, aspecto integrador, que permite educar a nuestros niños sobre los diferentes roles de los latinos en la sociedad americana y por supuesto sobre la diversidad cultural en todos los ámbitos de la vida diaria, mientras que los incentivamos a practicar el idioma español."

–Review at Mama XXI www.mamaxxi.com/buenas-noches-capitan-mama-book-tour/

. . . .

"El cuento ofrece una maravillosa oportunidad para que padres e hijos conversen sobre roles no tradicionales mientras aprenden a respetar el duro trabajo de nuestras fuerzas armadas."

–Mariela Dabbah, escritora de Find Your Inner Red Shoes,
founder of Red Shoe Movement

Marco rinsed his mouth, put his toothbrush inside his cup and dried his lips. The little boy turned off the light and grabbed White Pup, his blue and white sleeping buddy, from the shelf.

My ♥ is in the SKY

Marco se enjuagó la boca, puso su cepillo de dientes en el vasito y se secó los labios. El niño apagó la luz y agarró del estante a Cachorrito Blanco, su compañero de cama color azul y blanco.

Noticing his mama's bedroom door open, he peeked in. She was wearing a green costume he had seen many times before. Now he wanted to know more. He knocked on her door. "Yes, Sweetie?" she answered.

Al notar que la puerta de la recámara de su mamá estaba abierta, se asomó. Traía puesto un disfraz verde que él había visto antes varias veces. Ahora él quería saber más. Tocó la puerta. –¿Sí, cariño? –contestó ella.

"What are you wearing, Mama?" Marco asked. "This is my flight suit, love," she replied. "I wear it when I fly in the airplane at the Air Force base."

-¿Qué traes puesto, mamá? -preguntó Marco. -Este es mi traje de vuelo mi amor -respondió ella. -Me lo pongo cuando vuelo en el avión de la fuerza aérea.

"Why?" he asked. "A flight suit keeps me safe in the jet. It keeps me warm too," said Mama.

–¿Por qué? –preguntó el niño. –Un traje de vuelo me mantiene segura dentro del avión también me mantiene calientita –dijo mamá.

"What's this?" he asked, pointing to a square shape on her shoulders. "That's my rank. I am a Captain," Mama told him. "You're a Captain? Like the captain of a ship?" asked the little boy. "Yes, something like that sweetheart," she said with a smile.

-¿Qué es esto? -preguntó Marco -apuntando a una forma cuadrada en los hombros de ella. -Ese es mi rango. Soy Capitán -dijo mamá. -¿Eres Capitán? ¿Como el capitán de un barco? -preguntó el pequeño. -Si, algo así cariño -dijo ella con una sonrisa.

"What's this?" asked Marco, pulling off a colorful piece of her costume, smiling at the sound of detaching Velcro®. "That's my command patch," Mama explained. "Oh. What does that mean?" Marco wondered.

–¿Qué es esto? –preguntó Marco –arrancando una pieza colorida de su disfraz, sonriendo al escuchar el sonido que hace el Velcro® cuando se separa. –Ese es mi parche de mando –explicó mamá.
–Oh. ¿Qué significa eso? –preguntó Marco.

"It means I am part of a big team all over the world," Mama answered. "The group is called Air Mobility Command. We move people, fuel and things like trucks and food with our airplanes. These things are needed to keep the people of America and America's friends safe."

–Significa que soy parte de un equipo grande que abarca al mundo entero –contestó mamá. –Este grupo se llama Comando de Movilidad Aérea. Llevamos gente, combustible, cosas como camiones y comida en nuestros aviones. Estas cosas se necesitan para mantener seguros a la gente de nuestro país y a los amigos de nuestro país.

"What's this?" Marco asked, pulling the rectangular patch off her uniform. "That's my name tag with my wings," said Mama. "The wings identify my specific job in the flying world. I am an aircraft navigator. See the star on top?"

-¿Qué es esto? -preguntó Marco -jalando otro parche del uniforme. -Es mi nombre con mis alas -dijo mamá -Las alas identifican mi trabajo específico dentro del mundo aéreo. Soy un navegante aéreo. ¿Ves la estrella de arriba?

"Yes, I see it Mama," her son replied. "That means I have flown many hours in the KC-135 airplane," Mama told her little boy. "I teach others how to safely get airplanes together in the sky."

–Si, la veo mamá –respondió su hijo. –Eso quiere decir que he volado muchas horas en el avión KC-135 –dijo mamá. –Significa que también soy maestra y enseño a los demás a juntar aviones en el cielo de manera segura.

"Then, we connect our airplane to another military airplane in the air and give it the gas it needs to get to where it's going."

—Despues, conectamos nuestro avión a otro avión militar en el aire y le damos el combustible que necesita para llegar a su destino.

"The star is like a special prize for my wings. Do you like it?"
"Yes, Mama. It's very cool," Marco replied, feeling very proud
of his Mama.

—La estrella es como un premio especial para mis alas. ¿Te gusta?
—Sí, mamá. Me gusta mucho —respondió Marco —sintiéndose muy
orgulloso de su mamá.

"Mama, what's this patch that's red, white and blue?" He wanted to know. "That's my American flag," she replied. "Oh. What does it mean?" asked Marco.

-Mamá, ¿Qué es este parche rojo, blanco y azul? -pregunto Marco. -Es mi bandera Americana -respondió ella. -Oh. ¿Qué significa? -preguntó Marco.

"This is the symbol of our nation, the United States of America. I serve in our military to protect our country and to keep you safe," she replied.

—Este es el símbolo de nuestra nación, los Estados Unidos de América. Yo sirvo en nuestras fuerzas armadas para proteger a nuestro país y para mantenerte a ti seguro –respondió ella.

"What's the patch on this side, Mama?" Marco asked, grabbing the one with the bird. "That's my squadron patch," she answered. "The colors are of my team, the 96th Air Refueling Squadron. We fly out of Fairchild Air Force Base here in Spokane."

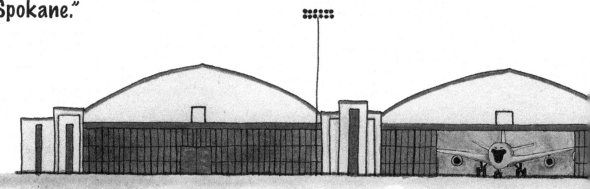

–¿Qué es el parche de este lado mamá? –preguntó Marco, refiriendose al parche con el dibujo de un pájaro. –Ese es el parche de mi escuadrón aéreo. Los colores son de mi equipo, El Escuadrón 96. Volamos de la base de la fuerza aérea aquí en Spokane –dijo ella.

"There are five different squadron teams here. Mine uses this patch, but sometimes I change it when I'm flying on the other side of the world," she explained to her little boy as she unzipped a pocket on her flight suit.

-Aquí hay cinco escuadrónes diferentes. El mío usa este parche, pero a veces lo cambio cuando estoy volando al otro lado del mundo -explicó ella a su pequeño abriendo un bolsillo de su traje de vuelo.

"When I come home from each trip, I have a new patch," she continued. "This one is from where I went last month—Souda Bay Naval Base on the Greek Island of Crete. When you're a bit older, we will visit some of these places together."

—Mira este parche —dijo mamá —Lo recibí cuando estuve en la base naval de la Bahía de Souda de la isla griega de Creta. Cuando estés un poco más grande mijito visitaremos algunos de estos lugares juntos.

"I miss you so much when you go away, Mama," said Marco, feeling sad.
"I miss you very much when I go away sweetheart," Mama agreed.
"But now it's time for bed, sweetie. Your sisters are already asleep,"
Mama told Marco. "Do you want to sleep with this special patch?"

-Te extraño mucho cuando te vas mamá -dijo Marco -sintiéndose triste.
-Yo tambien te extraño mucho cuando me voy cariño -dijo mamá.
-Pero ahora es tiempo de irse a la cama cariño. Tus hermanas ya estan
durmiendo -dijo mamá a Marco. -¿Quieres dormir con este parche
especial esta noche?

"Yes I do, Mama. Thank you!" Marco said happily. Mama put the patch over his heart. The Velcro stuck to his fleece pajamas! "Thanks for keeping me safe, Mama. Thanks to your team too," he said kissing his Mama.

–Sí mamá, gracias –dijo Marco entusiasmado. Mamá le puso el parche arriba del corazón. ¡El Velcro® se pegó a la tela de sus piyamas –Gracias por mantenernos seguros mamá y gracias a tu equipo también –dijo él besando a su mamá.

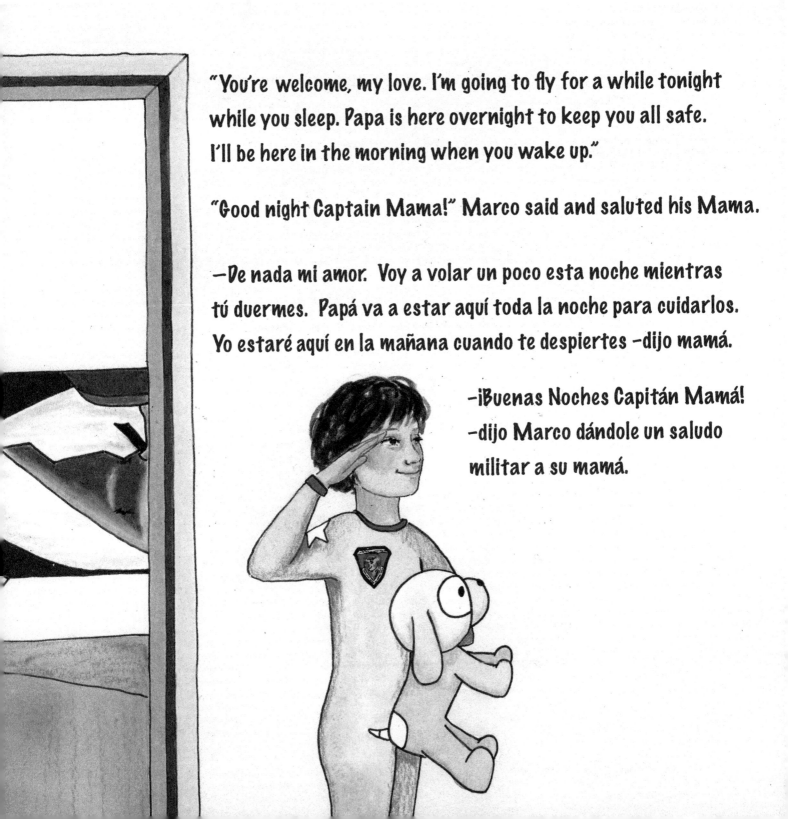

"You're welcome, my love. I'm going to fly for a while tonight while you sleep. Papa is here overnight to keep you all safe. I'll be here in the morning when you wake up."

"Good night Captain Mama!" Marco said and saluted his Mama.

—De nada mi amor. Voy a volar un poco esta noche mientras tú duermes. Papá va a estar aquí toda la noche para cuidarlos. Yo estaré aquí en la mañana cuando te despiertes –dijo mamá.

–¡Buenas Noches Capitán Mamá! –dijo Marco dándole un saludo militar a su mamá.

"Good night little man. I'll be right there to sing you a lullaby," she said while saluting the little boy and smiling.

–Buenas noches pequeño. Ahorita voy para cantarte una nana –dijo sonriendo con un saludo militar al niño.

Marco walked slowly backwards to his room, still looking at his Mama and holding White Pup.

Marco caminó lentamente para atrás a su cuarto, mirando a su mamá y con Cachorrito Blanco en sus brazos.

He climbed into his bed and touched her special patch stuck to his pajamas. As he waited for his lullaby, his thoughts were of feeling safe. He loved thinking about his Mama and her team, all wearing flight suits and wearing the same colors.

Se metió a su cama y tocó el parche especial que su mamá le había puesto. Mientras esperaba que le cantaran su nana, sus pensamientos eran de sentirse seguro. Le agradaba pensar en su mamá y en su equipo, todos con sus trajes de vuelo y todos vestidos con los mismos colores.

He loved learning about Mama's work on the airplanes. He would ask her if she could take him and his sisters to visit the airplane soon. He knew she'd smile and say "Yes!"

Le gustó aprender acerca del trabajo de su mamá con los aviones. Le preguntaría si podría llevarle con sus hermanas pronto a visitar el avión. Estaba seguro que con una sonrisa, ella diría que –¡Sí!

About the Author

This book was inspired by a conversation the author had with her son Kiyoshi the night before a Veterans Day event at his preschool. As Graciela donned her uniform, hat, scarf, patches and boots, her son entered the room on his way to bed when he spotted her in her "costume." His total curiosity and the questions he asked as he yanked each patch off the flight suit led Graciela to write the first draft of the manuscript that same night.

Photo by Rob Baker

Graciela Tiscareño-Sato is a graduate of the University of California at Berkeley. She completed the Aerospace Studies program as an AFROTC (Air Force Reserve Officer Training Program) scholarship cadet while earning her degree in Architecture and Environmental Design. During her active duty career in the U.S. Air Force, she deployed to four continents and dozens of countries as aircrew member, instructor and contingency planning officer. Flying many combat sorties over Southern Iraq in the NO FLY Zone after Operation Desert Storm earned her crew the prestigious Air Medal on her first deployment. Her favorite rendezvous for aerial refueling was with the SR-71 Blackbird as it came out of its high-altitude missions over the Earth at supersonic speeds.

She served with a NATO Battlestaff in Vicenza, Italy, as a military liaison officer at the U.S. Embassy in Quito, Ecuador and much more. She earned a Masters degree in International Management from the School of Global Commerce at Whitworth University in Spokane, Washington before leaving active service. After an international marketing management career with Siemens headquartered in Munich, Germany, she created her global marketing and publishing firm, Gracefully Global Group, LLC. In November 2010, she received "Entrepreneur of the Year" honors at the *LATINAStyle Magazine* Gala in Washington D.C.

Graciela actively mentors students who need education and career roadmaps, which is a central focus of her four-time award-winning and bestselling book, *Latinnovating*. As a journalist and blogger, her work has been published in the U.S. and Europe in a wide variety of media.

Graciela and her family live in the San Francisco Bay Area.

Contact Graciela and join the conversation about women in uniform at www.captainmama.com

About the Illustrator

Linda Lens first found her passion for art as a small child with her grandmother, Donna. She made art her passion since her first thunderstorm. Finding her talent, she has never stopped drawing. From crayons to oil paint, Linda has played with it all.

As a little girl, her mother would take her and her sister to the library where they would check out too many children's books. The beautiful illustrations and colors always fascinated Linda. From early on, one of her dreams was to become a children's book illustrator. Her love for capturing human expression followed her throughout college. She earned a degree in Studio Art, specializing in portraiture, from California State University in Hayward.

One of Linda's favorite quotes is from author Tom Robbins: "The purpose of art is to provide what life does not."

She lives with her son Johnny and daughter Saila, along with Cleo the black cat and two dogs, Shadow and Merlyn, somewhere near the ocean.

Contact Linda through the Contact Us tab at www.captainmama.com.

The author and illustrator met as their daughters attended Castro Valley Parent Nursery School together. Working there weekly as preschool parents, they entertained, taught and fed 25 three, four and five year-olds at a time. The idea of working together to create a children's book felt like a breeze after that experience!

Photo by Judy Rodriguez

ART ACTIVITY for Teachers and Parents to Lead

ADULTS: Please copy the patch outline on the following page. Children can design and decorate their own patches, just like those on Captain Mama's uniform, to represent their family, their pets, their school or a favorite team – whatever comes to mind.

Please photograph and share your favorite patch designs with us at Facebook.com/CaptainMama. If you'd like, we can connect you with the company that made the embroidered patches for us so you can have some real patches made too!

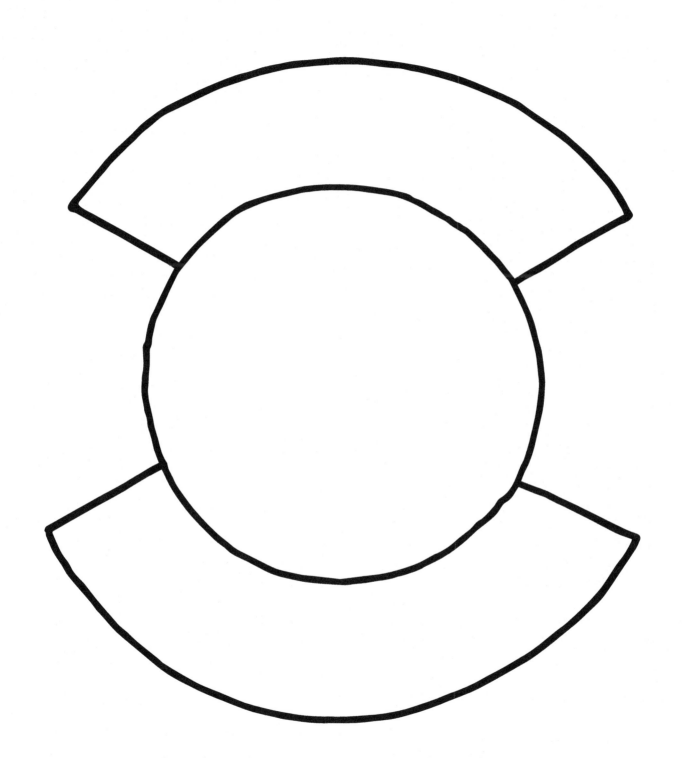

Links to Cool Stuff

The author and her children at the Women in Military Service for America Memorial reading mommy's service highlights.

They'll be able to take their kids there too.

WOMEN IN MILITARY SERVICE FOR AMERICA MEMORIAL (WIMSA)

Do you know a woman who is serving in the military now? Perhaps you know a woman veteran? Please have her become a permanent part of this living memorial at the entrance to Arlington National Cemetery in Virginia. She'll become part of history!

www.womensmemorial.org/Membership/reg.html

GIRLS WITH WINGS INC. (GWW)

With a tagline of "Girls need flight plans not fairy tales," GWW is a uniquely creative organization that "uses aviation to encourage girls to reach their full potential by introducing young girls to their role models in aviation-related careers and hobbies." Stories of today's women aviators abound; check it out and be sure to meet the adorable Penelope Pilot character.

www.girlswithwings.com

VISIT WWW.CAPTAINMAMA.COM TO:

→ Write to the author and her son, and ask questions.
→ Print patch outlines to design a patch for your event or team.
→ Get your very own embroidered patch of the book's cover art.
→ AND MORE...

Dedicated to the Fairchild AFB crew of Shell 77.

Thank you for your service.

Captain Mark "Tyler" Voss

Captain Victoria "Tori" Pinckney, a true Captain Mama

Tech Sergeant Herman "Tre" Mackey III

CPSIA information can be obtained
at www.ICGtesting.com
Printed in the USA
LVOW06s0559190416

484205LV00006B/7/P

3 1901 05731 6236